Dieter

sometimes it's TURKEY-
sometimes it's FEATHERS

by LORNA BALIAN

ABINGDON PRESS   NASHVILLE

SOMETIMES IT'S TURKEY—
SOMETIMES IT'S FEATHERS

Copyright © 1973   by Abingdon Press

Ninth Printing 1987

This book is printed on acid-free paper.

Library of Congress Cataloging in Publication Data

BALIAN, LORNA
    Sometimes it's turkey—sometimes it's feathers.
    SUMMARY: When she finds a turkey egg, Mrs. Gumm
    decides to hatch it and have a turkey for Thanksgiving
    dinner.
    [1. Thanksgiving Day—Stories] I. Title.
    PZ7.B1978So   [E]   72-3867

ISBN 0-687-37106-6

Previously published under ISBN 0–687–39074-5

MANUFACTURED BY THE PARTHENON PRESS AT
NASHVILLE, TENNESSEE, UNITED STATES OF AMERICA

For Blanche "Na" Eisenacher
who talks with the animals

Little old Mrs. Gumm found an egg.

She was hunting for wild mushrooms,
and there on the ground,
nearly hidden in a messy nest of leaves,
was a large cream-colored egg—
with freckles.

Yes, indeed!
An egg with freckles.
"Imagine!"

She filled her mushroom basket
with soft new April grass,
placed the egg gently in the center,

and hurried home with her treasure.

Mrs. Gumm was so excited
she almost stepped on Cat,
who was sleeping on the steps.

"Wake up, Cat," she said.
"Wake up and look at our Thanksgiving dinner!
An egg, Cat. A freckled egg!
A genuine turkey egg, I do believe!"

"We'll try to hatch it, Cat," she said,
covering the egg with a soft piece of flannel
and setting it in a warm place.

"We'll hatch it and feed it
and let it grow plump.
What a fine Thanksgiving dinner we will have.
Imagine!"

For days and days they watched it.
Watched it and turned it and warmed it,
until finally, one day in May
they heard a "tap . . . tap . . . tap."
And there on the freckled shell was a tiny crack.

"Tap . . . tap . . . tap . . . tap, tap, tap."
And the crack became a tiny hole.
They watched and listened,
listened and watched . . .
"It's hatching, Cat," said Mrs. Gumm.
"Oh! What a fine Thanksgiving dinner we will have."

It was a sticky, wet, boney little lump
that tumbled out of the cracked, freckled shell.
As it dried it became a fuzzy little lump
with beady black eyes and a sharp beak.

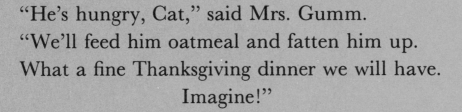

"He's hungry, Cat," said Mrs. Gumm.
"We'll feed him oatmeal and fatten him up.
What a fine Thanksgiving dinner we will have.
Imagine!"

Did that turkey eat!
He ate everything in sight!
Oatmeal,
Wheaties,
cornmeal and bread,
seeds,
nuts,
insects,
sand,
and cat food.

Did that turkey grow!
"Turkey's growing fast, Cat," said Mrs. Gumm.
"He'll be plenty big for Thanksgiving dinner."

In June, while Mrs. Gumm was planting seeds,
Turkey was eating the strawberries.
While Mrs. Gumm was looking for strawberries,
Turkey was eating as many seeds as he could find.

"Never mind, Cat," said Mrs. Gumm.
"The more he eats, the plumper he gets,
and what a fine Thanksgiving dinner we will have.
Imagine!"

Turkey ate raspberries in July.
Red raspberries, black raspberries,
white, unripe raspberries—
green peas, inchworms, grass seeds—and cat food.

"Tsk, tsk, Cat," said Mrs. Gumm.
"Raspberry jam would have been tasty
with our Thanksgiving dinner,
but at least there will be plenty of turkey."

The grapes grew sweet and purple in August,
and Turkey ate them—
grapes, lima beans, caterpillars, pea gravel—
and cat food.

"There will be no grape jelly this year, Cat,"
said Mrs. Gumm,
"but what a big, plump Thanksgiving turkey we will have.
Imagine!"

The September wind blew the thorn apples off the tree,
and Turkey gobbled them up as fast as they fell.
Thorn apples, weed seeds, grasshoppers, ladybugs—
and cat food.

"My, my," said Mrs. Gumm.
"Have you ever seen a plumper bird than that, Cat?
What a fine Thanksgiving dinner we will have."

Mrs. Gumm shelled corn in October.
Turkey helped and Cat watched.

"The corn will make him tasty and tender, Cat.
My, what a delicious Thanksgiving dinner we will have."

Preparations for Thanksgiving Day began
early in November.
Mrs. Gumm found the hatchet—
and ground some corn for cornbread.
She sharpened the hatchet—
and cooked cranberry sauce.
She honed the hatchet—
and baked pumpkin pie.
She polished the hatchet—
and mixed up an onion-and-chestnut stuffing.

She picked up the sharp, honed, polished hatchet
and said, "Wait here, Cat. It's time to prepare
that big, fat Turkey.
What a fine Thanksgiving dinner we will have!"

What a feast!
Cornbread, all warm and crumbly.
Bright red, sticky sweet cranberry sauce.
Spicy, golden pumpkin pie.
A steaming bowl of fragrant onion-and-chestnut stuffing—
and cat food.

"Sit right down, Cat," said Mrs. Gumm.
"I'll bring that nice plump Turkey to the table.
What a fine Thanksgiving this will be!"

"I have so much to be thankful for," said Mrs. Gumm.
"A Thanksgiving feast,
and two good friends to share it with.
Imagine!"

"He'll be bigger—and much plumper—next Thanksgiving,"
said little old Mrs. Gumm.
"IMAGINE!"